GW00731413

One sunny spring morning, a young fox, brown of colour decided to go for a walk.
He was like no other fox as he was a runt, smaller than the other foxes with larger ears
and a paw that was slightly smaller than the rest.

Upon his walk, as he trod further
and further through the woods he heard some strange sounds.
Now, being a fox you would think he is used to strange sounds but he
had never heard this sound before.
It was like a rustling and the crunching of leaves that didn't seem to
stop even when he called out hello.

1

As he looked, more and more worried with anticipation,
he saw a small bush in front of him.

He looked closely and what he saw was strange.

It was like a worm but green and had legs.
The fox thought he was dreaming.
He took one more step, the small creature screamed
and hid behind a leaf.

The fox said, "hello I'm Freddie what's your name?"
the small creature still slightly shaking pulled away from her leaf and
worriedly said
"my, my name iii-is candy oh please don't eat me Mr Fox"
hiding behind her leaf again.

Freddie looked at her confused and said
"I'm not going to eat you I want to be your friend"

The slightly confused Candy pulled away the leaf from her face
slightly and said
"you want to be friends with me?"

Freddie said, "Well I don't have many friends the other foxes
think I'm funny because I'm the runt and have a
slightly smaller front paw and my ears are bigger than everyone
else's and I'm smaller than them too so I want to make some friends."

Candy agreed to be his friend. She told him
"I get lonely in wintertime as my only friend Barney the bear
hibernates so would love to have another friend all year round."

Freddie told candy to get on his head and she did.

As they were strolling through the woods Freddie said
"Candy what sort of animal are you?"

Candy said, "well I'm a caterpillar silly fox".
Freddie replied "oh I have never seen a caterpillar before
I was a little scared when you screamed".

Candy laughed, "I was scared when I saw you I have
never been this close to a fox before".

Freddie responded, "why? I'm not scary".

Candy said "well I heard that foxes eat caterpillars so
we have to avoid foxes at all cost".

Freddie answered "that's not true we don't eat caterpillars
because I heard they are too small and have a horrible
noise that must have been your scream" they both laughed
and carried on walking through the woods.

Realising that they cannot always believe everything they
hear and should figure others out themselves.

Orange light shone brightly over the trees as the sun started to set in the forest.
Freddie said, "I think we should head back home now where do you live Candy?"

Candy said, "the smallest tree in the woods is where I live".
Freddie looked puzzled and questioned her by saying "is that a real place?"
Candy said, "yes Freddie now come on keep going we are almost there".

As the pair continued to walk, they swerved around a tree and there
it was, the smallest tree in the woods.

It was very beautiful.
It had yellow, red, and white flowers on it and was about the size of half a house.
Between the beautiful flowers, Freddie saw a little, caterpillar-sized door.

Freddie lowered himself to the floor, Candy jumped off his head,
and Freddie said, "can we do this tomorrow?"
Candy said, "yes, of course, we can do this every day."

Freddie cheered and they said goodbye and
Freddie headed home to go to sleep.

The next day Freddie walked over to Candy's house
and waited for her.

She came out and said
"hi Freddie I was worried you weren't coming at first"

Freddie said "oh sorry I'm slow because of my paw this
is why I can't go outside at night as the other foxes do"

Candy replied to him "awwww I'm sorry, but hey,
if you went out at night you would have never met me"

Freddie smiled a big smile and said
"that's right and now I have a best friend".

As the two friends were walking through the woods candy said
"I'm a little hungry can we stop and eat something?"
Freddie said, "of course where would you like to stop?"
Candy answered him, sighing and putting her hand on her head.
"anywhere I just need a big juicy leaf"

Freddie said "big juicy leaf got it"

So off Freddie set to try and find the biggest,
juiciest leaf he could find in the woods.

He remembered from a past walk seeing the most green,
beautiful, juiciest leaves,
Freddie said, "I know just the place".

So the two set to find the bush.
The bush was surrounded by enormous trees that made
the leaves stay green and juicy all year round without falling off.

Upon arrival, Candy looked up and noticed the bush she couldn't
wait to eat all the leaves and she looked at the bush in shock,
with a smile and drooling slightly.

Candy was so thrilled that she couldn't even say thank you to Freddie.
She just mumbled some letters, Freddie giggled and said
"dig in" as he lowered his head to the bush.

After an hour of leaf-munching, Candy came away very happy and said
"Freddie that was amazing thank you"

Freddie was so pleased with himself that he helped her out that after
he dropped her home he headed into the woods
to see what other treats he could find for her.

The next morning came around and Freddie had left early to
get to Candy's house.

She was surprised to see him so early,
before she could even say hello Freddie said
"I have a surprise for you jump on"
Candy sounding confused said "ok?"
and jumped on his head.

Freddie was so excited to show her the surprise he tried to run and tripped because of his small paw.

He stopped and shouted "Candy?"
she answered him and said
"I'm still here are you ok? Did you hurt yourself?"

Freddie feeling relieved said "phew no I'm fine forgot about my paw.
I really wanted to show you the surprise but I am not quick enough"

He then had a sad look on his face looking down to the ground
like when clouds look down before it rains.
Candy walked onto his nose and looked in his eyes to say
"hey I'm sure it's a great surprise it doesn't matter how long it takes
as long as I have my best friend with me that's all that matters".

Freddie smiled and they set off to the surprise.
As they approached Freddie told Candy to close her eyes.
She questioned him "why do I need to close my eyes?"

Freddie told her "because all the best surprises are better
when you don't get a glimpse of it first"

Candy agreed to
close her eyes and Freddie strolled her to the surprise.

She opened her eyes to Freddie's remark and what was presented
in front of her was the biggest berry tree in the woods Candy said
"oh thank you berries are my favourite how did you know"

Freddie said "just a lucky guess"

Now this was not any normal berry bush this had the brightest red berries that glistened in the sun and the leaves were the perfect shade of green and Candy ate nearly the whole bush Freddie noticed and said "How can a small animal like you eat all the berries?"

Candy said, "I don't know I was just hungry?" and after that, every day Candy became more and more hungry.

She was eating all the leaves on bushes and trees and anything she could find. Every day she got bigger the more she ate.

Freddie began to worry about her but every time he asked if she
was ok her reply was just "I'm fine I'm just hungry"

So Freddie didn't say anything else because he wanted his
best friend still and didn't want to make her upset
with all the questions.

The seasons were starting to change and storms tore across
the forest destroying everything in its path.

Months passed and the woods grew colder Candy's home was
torn down in a strong wind of the storm and now she had
nowhere to go.

She wanted to go and find her best friend but she realised
she never found out where he lived so she set off in the
cold snowy storm to find her friend.

She looked everywhere for him high and low.

She was about to give up when she found bits of old wood and rocks,
piled on top of each other which made
Freddie's small cave.

Candy went to go in, she was cold and frozen but stopped at
the entrance and just stood there. In front of the stone
doorway was a small opening she wormed her way in and
was staring into the darkness.

She didn't know what she would be faced with and so she
edged her way through the cave hoping to find her friend.
As she got deeper into the cave she heard breathing,
lots of breathing, foxes breathing.

She remembered what she had heard
"foxes eat caterpillars do not go near them"
then just as she was about to turn around
and leave she heard another voice in her head say
"foxes don't eat caterpillars we thought you were scary".

So she continued her journey through the cave
and she came across lots of foxes huddled together asleep.
She saw a small fox on his own,
slightly away from the pack, sleeping by himself.

As Candy approached this fox she recognised the ears and as the fox
rolled over it was the same small paw of her best friend.

She rushed over to him and he asked her what she was doing there.

Candy told him everything and Freddie agreed she could
stay with him until the storm was over.

She rested under his tail and by his body to keep warm.

The 3-day storm was finally over and Freddie woke up early to go on a
walk with Candy so he woke her up and they set off.

Freddie was determined to find her a new home so off they
went for hours trying to find a new home.

Even with lots of snack stops on the way as
Candy was more hungry than ever.

As they got near the lake Candy said "wait, stop, go back"
Freddie asked "what? what is it?"
and there it was Candy's perfect home.

It was a stump of an old tree and was very spacious on the inside.
It was surrounded by mushrooms and little white daisies.

Above it grew two big tulips that were a shade
of pink that candy and Freddie didn't know existed.

They were big, bright, and beautiful and they
knew it was Candy's new home.

The pair of them were inseparable.
Everyday Freddie travelled to meet Candy even though it
was a little further than last time he still travelled to her.

But one bright sunny morning Freddie got to
candy's house and waited for her but she never showed up.

He stuck his nose inside her house,
"Candy?" he cried but nobody responded.

He remembered how big she was getting
and thought maybe she is slow like himself
but he waited all day and she never showed up.

Freddie went back every day for 5 days and
it was the same thing that happened.

Candy didn't answer or show.

On the last day, Freddie went home crying along
the way as he thought maybe she didn't want to be
his friend anymore so he stayed in his cave for two days upset.

Whilst in the cave a few of the other foxes noticed that Freddie wasn't
his usual happy self and that he hadn't gone for a walk in two days.

So they decided to ask him why.

Freddie said "why do you want to know it's not like
you let me join in with your games or your night travels".

The other foxes said
"that's because you would slow us down with your paw.
We want to take you but it's dangerous"
and they walked away laughing.

They were always acting kind to Freddie then they would push him away and
always try to push him over and often succeeded because of his paw.

Freddie never let it get to him he would often get up and walk away and
the other foxes would laugh and say "aww are you going to go cry now"
and Freddie used to cry but doesn't anymore.

Freddie's mum walked over and said to him
"Are they giving you trouble?"
Freddie said in a sad mopey voice "no"
his mum then said
"So what's up? You haven't been outside in two days"

Freddie explained the whole story of how he
met candy and what had happened.

His mum smiled and said
"I think you should go and find her again
you may just be surprised and she may be looking for you".

Freddie hesitated and his mum said,
"go on go look for her and have fun".

So Freddie set off with his head down looking sad and gloomy.
He got to his best friend's house and just collapsed and
laid down outside and didn't call her or
anything he just sat there hoping but not feeling confident.

But out of the blue these big, purple, velvet wings,
with black lines that outlined all the patterns, gleamed in the sun.

A blinding purple light shone down onto
the ground causing Freddie to cover his eyes.

He asked worriedly "who are you?"

29

The purple butterfly answered
"you don't even recognise your best friend?"
Freddie jumped up in the air with excitement and said
"wow, you've changed candy!"

Candy said "yes, I understand everything now this is why I was always hungry
and why I disappeared for a week I'm so sorry Freddie but now
I'm back for good we can continue our adventures".

The two best friends; Freddie the fox and Candy Butterfly headed
toward the river and rested on the bank,
Freddie said "when you were gone I thought you didn't want to be my friend anymore"

Candy said "I thought the same when you didn't come to find me for two days"

They both stared at the river and all they could hear
was the sound of the river and all the buzzing bugs around them.

They both turned to each other and said sorry.

Candy flew onto Freddie's nose and hugged him.

It was such a special moment for the friends that they both closed their eyes and sighed with closure that everything was forgiven and forgotten.

Freddie was overwhelmed with happiness.

The End

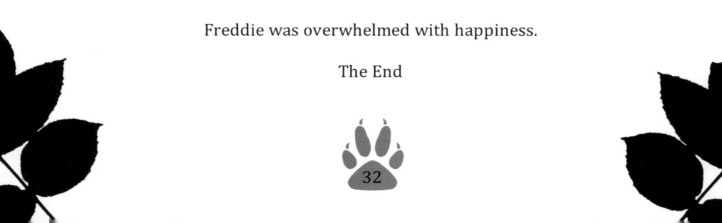